D0910142

ITALIAN PEEPSHOW

Books by

Eleanor Farjeon

THE NEW BOOK OF DAYS

TEN SAINTS

MARTIN PIPPIN IN THE APPLE ORCHARD

MARTIN PIPPIN IN THE DAISY FIELD

THE SILVER CURLEW

THE GLASS SLIPPER

GRANNIE GRAY

PERKIN THE PEDLAR

THE LITTLE BOOKROOM

THE CHILDREN'S BELLS

TALES FROM CHAUCER

JIM AT THE CORNER

Eleanor Farjeon

ITALIAN PEEPSHOW

Illustrated by
Edward Ardizzone

London
OXFORD UNIVERSITY
PRESS

Oxford University Press, Amen House, London E.C.4

GLASGOW NEW YORK TORONTO MELBOURNE WELLINGTON
BOMBAY CALCUTTA MADRAS KARACHI KUALA LUMPUR
CAPE TOWN IBADAN NAIROBI ACCRA

First published in the United States by Frederick A. Stokes Company, 1926

First published in this edition 1960

Reprinted 1961

PRINTED IN GREAT BRITAIN BY
WESTERN PRINTING SERVICES LTD BRISTOL

FOR

Bridget and Chloe and Nan

FOR WHOM THIS BOOK BEGAN

Contents

I	BRIDGET IN ITALY	1
II	ORANGES AND LEMONS	8
III	THE BIRTHDAY CARNIVAL	19
IV	ROSAURA'S BIRTHDAY	27
V	ANINA	45
VI	THE KING OF TRIPOLI BRINGS THE PASTA	51
VII	NAN AND CECCHINO	63
VIII	THE HERB OF FEAR	69
IX	NELLA'S DANCING SHOES	79
X	GOOD-BYE TO ITALY	89
XI	THE STORY OF MR AND MRS RINGDALY	91

I

BRIDGET IN ITALY

Bridget has lived in a lot of different places, and no matter where she has lived I have sometimes lived there too, and told her stories, and had parties, and picnics, and fun of all sorts.

First she lived in Wisbech, which is as flat as a pancake, and surrounded by apple-trees as far as you can see. On a spring day men sit in the apple-trees painting them white all over, and under the apple-trees grow miles and miles of tulips and daffodils, like strips of red and yellow ribbon.

Another time Bridget lived in Pangbourne, where the *Majestic* steamed up and down the river, and we sat in the hay-houses we made on the banks and waved to it as it went by.

But especially Bridget lived in Italy, so presently I went to Italy too to find out what they did there.

In Italy things are quite different.

Bridget lived in a villa on the top of a hill, and down in the valley was a beautiful city cut in half by a green river, and so full of palaces and domes and towers that it was like a king's city. The city had a girl's name. It was called Florence.

All down the hillside there were trees, but you would not find such trees in Wisbech or in Pangbourne. The trees were little low grey olive-trees, like round puffs of smoke, and straight stiff black cypresses, like tall chimneys. You might almost think the cypresses had puffed up the olive-trees.

Among the trees were houses, but they were

different too; they were square houses with sharp corners and square turrets. Some of them were all white, and some were painted up and down in blue-

and-white stripes, and others were painted round and round in red-and-yellow stripes, and nearly all of them had green wooden shutters. They looked like big toys taken out of a box; and they also looked like big boxes out of which you might take the most delightful toys. Most of them had courtyards and terraces where orange- and lemon-trees grew in big green tubs. The oranges hung among the dark green leaves like a lot of little suns, but the lemons were paler and clearer, like the yellow moon.

One day in spring we went to an olive-farm a little way down the hill. "We" means a lot of people as well as Bridget and me. This time it meant Bridget's Mummy, and Ivy who is Bridget's nurse, and Chloe and Nan, who are Bridget's littler sisters, though Bridget is little herself. It also meant Gianina and Vuv-Vuv, who are Bridget's and Chloe's dolls. Gianina is rag with black wool hair and wires inside her, so that you can twist her legs and arms into any position you like. She came from Ravenna in the marshes on the other side of Italy. Vuv-Vuv who is much older is also rag, but she is bigger and softer and has no wires; she is just for cuddling. She has boot-button eyes, and beautiful pink cheeks, and a calm happy smile, and curls, all of which, except the eyes, are painted on her face by Chloe's Mummy. Every now and then she has a bath, and new pink cheeks and curls, and a new smile, are painted on when she is dry, but she is always the same Vuv-Vuv, only a little more beautiful each time. She looks rather like Chloe, who is her mother.

We went through the farm gate, past the white farm with its oranges and lemons, looking like a house for a prince, and down the slopes into the olive-orchard. In the olive-trees men were sitting, singing and whistling like birds. Under the olive-trees the small black olives from last year still lay scattered among the new green corn that was springing up, though it was only February. But in Italy there are wild roses when in England there is fog. The olives looked like little withered plums.

"Taste one!" said Bridget.

I tasted one—oh! it *was* bitter! I made a face, and Bridget and Chloe laughed.

But among the corn were lovelier things than olives; there were big purple anemones, and golden aconites, and along the low stone walls were bright wild marigolds and millions of daisies; and at the bottom of the orchard, hanging over a wide, shallow, stony stream, full of big grey stones round which the water brawled in a white froth and made paddling-pools, there were pink roses, smooth and cup-like; and in one part there were lavender bushes growing from the walls, and in other parts there were blue grape-hyacinths to be found—these were great treasures to add to Bridget's and Chloe's bunches. Bridget and Chloe ran about the orchard finding new flowers, and we lay in the grass making daisy-chains for Nan, who picked daisies close off by their heads to put in the chains; and the men sang in the trees.

When Bridget and Chloe were tired, they made houses under the olive-trees, with twisty doorways in and out between the trees and the walls, and we visited them and had tea with their dolls. Presently we felt evening coming, and it was time to go.

As we went up the terraces we saw the biggest moon we had ever seen rise very slowly behind a castle on a high hill, and we watched it until it swam clear in the air. A man in a tree near by was whistling away and watching it too.

"How big the moon is tonight!" called Bridget's Mummy.

"Yes, yes," called the man gaily, "and if the earth were a little nearer the moon would be a little bigger!" And he went on whistling and we went away.

On the road home we saw a green lizard run out of a crack in the wall to feel the sun, for the sun was in the sky as well as the moon, and the green Italian lizards love the sun. We saw it gleam like a jewel. But when it knew we were near, it scuttled away and vanished into another crack like a fairy. After this Bridget and Chloe ran along the road to sit Gianina and Vuv-Vuv in cracks in the wall, and then ran back to tell us to look for fairies. As we drew near we crept towards the doll-fairies with our hats, like boys trying to catch butterflies, and—

Presto! Now I have you, Gianina!

Ecco! Now I have you, Vuv-Vuv!

But when the hats were opened, the fairies were not there! Had they vanished into the cracks also? Could little people go where lizards went? Suddenly, at a little distance ahead, there they were again, sitting in the wall. It was very mysterious.

When we got home, it was bedtime.

At bedtime there are always stories, and I will tell you some of those stories later on. But the story that comes next was never told to Bridget and Chloe in Italy. It has been waiting till now.

II

ORANGES AND LEMONS

There was once a Prince who grew oranges and lemons in a white palace on the Italian hills. All over the hills there were palaces of other princes who also grew oranges and lemons, blue-and-white palaces and red-and-yellow palaces, but the Prince in the white palace grew the biggest fruit because he lived highest up the hill, and his trees caught the most sun. The Blue-and-White Prince and the Red-and-Yellow Prince came to visit him, followed by their pages carrying their best orange- and lemon-trees in green tubs, and when they reached the courtyard of the White Prince they put their trees down beside his and looked from one to the other. Then they shook their heads sadly and said:

"Yes! Yours are the biggest!"

And they went down the hill again, with their pages carrying the tubs behind them.

But on the very top of the hill there was a black castle with a tall tower, and in it lived a Princess whom nobody had ever seen. Every evening at sunset she came and stood on the top of her tower and looked at the sun going down and the moon coming up; and one evening the Prince got his telescope, and instead of looking through it at the sun and the moon, he looked at the Princess. She was all in black, and she wore a black mask on her face, so that even the White Prince could say no more than other people that he had seen her.

He went into his olive-orchard and called Beppe, his man, who sat whistling in a tree like a bird.

"Beppe," said the White Prince, "you must go to the castle on the hill, and ask the Black Princess to come down and look at my oranges and lemons."

"It shall be done," said Beppe, and up the hill he went, whistling like a bird.

Before long he came back again.

"What does she say?" asked the White Prince.

"She says," said Beppe, "that she has no need to look at your oranges and lemons, because she has bigger and finer ones of her own."

"I don't believe it!" said the White Prince. "Go back and ask her if I may come and see her oranges and lemons, and if they are really bigger than mine I will give her my palace and all that is in it."

"It shall be done," said Beppe, and up the hill he went, whistling like a bird.

Before long he came back again.

"What does she say?" asked the White Prince.

"She says," said Beppe, "that she will not let any-one look at her oranges and lemons who can't find his way in for himself; but she will put her trees upon the castle wall, and you can look at them through your telescope if you like. If you don't like, you needn't."

The White Prince got red then, because he knew she had seen him staring at her through the telescope while she was looking at the sky. To hide his confusion he said:

"How did you find *your* way into the castle? The way you got in, I can get in."

"I didn't," said Beppe. "I called through the keyhole and she called back."

So *that* was no help.

"Did you look through the keyhole?" he asked next.

"I did," said Beppe.

"And what does she look like?"

"She wore her black mask," said Beppe.

So *that* was no help.

That evening, when the Black Princess came as usual to the top of her tower to watch the sun going down and the moon coming up, she carried in her arms two little green tubs, which she set on the wall where the White Prince could see them. But when he looked through his telescope he saw nothing in the tubs but two little trees with glossy green leaves, and on one was a lime and on the other a tangerine.

Then he got very annoyed with her for making game of him, and he called Beppe to him and said:

"Go to the Black Princess and say that her fruit is almost too small to be seen."

"It shall be done," said Beppe, and up the hill he went, whistling like a bird, and back he came again in no time.

"What does she say?" asked the White Prince.

"She says," said Beppe, "that you must have looked at her fruit through the wrong end of the telescope. And she says that if you were a little nearer, the fruit would look a little bigger."

This made the Prince so cross that he didn't sleep all night. In the morning he went up the hill to the Black Castle himself, and when he got there he banged on the door.

"Who is there?" called a sweet voice from the other side.

"The Prince of Oranges and Lemons!" said he.

"Oh, I know you now!" said the voice. "But I think you are only the Prince of Limes and Tangerines. What do you want?"

"I want to come in!"

"Find the way in!" said she. And no more would she say.

Downhill he went empty-handed, and uphill he came with his key. But his key was too big, and her keyhole too small.

Downhill he went with his key, and uphill he came with his ladder. But her wall was too high, and his ladder was too short.

Downhill he went with his ladder, and uphill he came with his cannon. But her gate was too strong, and his shot was too weak.

Then he sat down in despair by the wall, and said, "There is no way in!"

"There are a hundred ways in!" laughed a tiny voice by his ear.

He looked round to see who had spoken, but there was nobody there; only the insects humming in the sun, and the green lizards basking on the walls. As he turned his head his shadow fell on the nearest one, and it scuttled into a crack like a fairy.

He looked at the crack, and at the hundred other cracks in the wall, each of which was a way in for a lizard.

"Oh! If only I were no bigger than a lizard!" cried the Prince.

"That's easy enough!" laughed the tiny voice by his ear. "Go and get your telescope."

Downhill he went with his cannon, and uphill he came with his telescope.

"What next?" asked the Prince.

"Stand by a crack in the wall," said the tiny voice, "and point the telescope at yourself."

"Which end of the telescope?" asked the Prince.

"The end that makes you look little, of course!"

So the Prince pointed the wrong end of the telescope at a crack in the wall, and stood himself between the telescope and the crack. As quick as a wink he grew as small as a lizard, and slipped through the crack like a fairy. Then he ran with all his tiny might up the Black Tower, and came out on the turret just as the moon was coming up and the sun going down. There, like a giantess, stood the Black Princess, watching them through her mask.

The Prince tugged at her skirt crying, "Here I am! Here I am! I have found the way in!"

The Princess looked down and down until she saw him and said, "So you have, my Prince of Lizards! It only remains for you to tell me what you think of my oranges and lemons." And she pointed to the wall, where stood the two biggest trees in the two most monstrous tubs that the Prince had ever seen, and on one hung an orange as big as the sun, and on the other a lemon as big as the moon.

The Prince looked at them for a long while, shook his head sadly, and said, "Yes! Yours are the biggest."

"In that case," said she, "you must give me your palace and all that is in it."

"A promise is a promise," said the Prince. "But first take off your mask."

She did so, and when the black mask was removed the Prince saw that her face was as beautiful as the sun by day and the moon by night. She let the mask lie where it fell, and picking up the Prince with one hand and her trees with the other, came out of the castle for the very first time. When she saw the telescope lying on the ground, she picked that up, too, and went downhill to the Prince's palace.

She set down the trees and the Prince and the telescope in the middle of the floor and looked all round her, and said, "It is a beautiful palace, and I am glad it is mine."

"It is yours with all that is in it," said the Prince. "If you take it you must take me, too. A promise is a promise."

"But you are almost too small to be seen!" said she.

"You are looking through the wrong end of the telescope," said the Prince. "If you come a little nearer I will look a little bigger."

So she came a little nearer, and as she did so he placed himself in front of the right end of the telescope. As quick as a wink he grew as big as a man. By the time the Princess had reached him, she had stopped looking like a giantess, and was just as small as a woman. And on the floor he saw two trees that were tiny enough to be carried in one hand, and on one was a lime and on the other a tangerine.

"Are those the trees you showed me up in your castle?" asked the Prince.

"To be sure they are," said she, "and very fine trees, too. Nobody in Italy has bigger fruit than I have."

The Prince gave her a kiss and said, "Very well! Let us come out and look at *my* orange- and lemon-trees, and bring yours with you."

They went out on the terrace where his beautiful fruit-trees stood in their tubs, and the fruit shone gold and yellow in the sunset and the moonrise. The Prince made the Princess put down her little tubs beside his big ones, and said:

"Beppe shall judge, once and for all."

Then he called to his man, who was sitting in an olive-tree watching the sky from the orchard below.

"Beppe! Which are the biggest, hers or mine?"

But Beppe, instead of looking at the fruit on the trees, looked like a stupid at the sun and moon in the sky, and said, "Hers are," and went on whistling like a bird.

There was nothing more to be done but for the Prince and Princess to get married. And so they did.

III

THE BIRTHDAY CARNIVAL

One day it was my birthday.

It was soon after the Carnival, when grown-up people and little boys and girls all put on fancy costumes and ran about the streets. Some of the dresses were beautiful, and some were just coloured rags, but they were all gay; and so were the hearts of the people who wore them. Some of them tooted trumpets and rattled tambourines. Those who could afford them wore satin masks, white and green and pink and black and scarlet. Those who could afford less, wore calico masks. Those who could afford nothing, wore none. And their grimy little faces were as bright with smiles as their companions' were with calico and satin. A few wore long noses. Beautiful ladies with hidden faces rode about in carriages decked with garlands of flowers, and waved their tambourines and ribbons as they went by. The masked children danced and ran and leaped about the big square and the old market, looking like the little puppets which can be bought everywhere in Italy, in all sizes—as long as your forearm or as short as your finger. The puppets have long wires fastened to their heads, by which you can make them dance. A bunch of little ones hang by their wires on a nail in Bridget's and Chloe's house. All the puppets have their special well-known names: Harlequin, Columbine, Brighella, Donna Laura, Scaramouch, The King, The Queen, The Doctor, Florindo, Rosaura, Sten-torello, and twenty more. The children in the

Carnival were like the puppets come to life in the streets. If they caught you they teased you and kissed you, pinched you, petted you, and begged for halfpennies; and they talked in high piping voices so that you should not guess who they were. All this was in Siena, a day's journey from Florence.

When we got back to Florence, on the eve of my birthday, we were still thinking about the Carnival.

Bridget and Chloe and their Mummy said, "We will give you a Carnival Birthday Party, and you mustn't come into the drawing-room till tea-time."

Bridget and her Mummy were shut up a long time in the drawing-room, getting it ready. Chloe was not very well, and could not help.

We all went apart to think about our dresses. The dresses were great secrets. I thought I would go as Scaramouch—a sort of coloured clown. I was half in red and half in blue, with one purple stocking and one of turquoise. I made a tall clown's hat of newspaper, and criss-crossed it with ribbons, and stuck it with rosettes; my mask was black satin with pink ribbons, and I carried a rolling-pin for a stick—it was nearly as tall as myself, for it was the pin with which they roll out the Pasta till it can be cut into strips a yard long and more. Pasta is the name for all the different sorts of macaroni which the Italians eat; there are more sorts than you have fingers and thumbs, but I will tell you about them another time.

When I was ready I waited until a voice called, "You can come now!"

I went into the drawing-room, and what did I see? The blinds were drawn down, and the room was hung with streamers of many-coloured paper, drooping in chains from point to point, a sort of fairy spider's web floating above my head. It hung in the light and disappeared in the shadows; for the only spots of light in the room were made by the coloured candles on the birthday tea-table, shining on the almond and raisin cakes, the cream tarts, and the sweetmeats. The corners of the long room were left full of shadows; and round the tea-table, in strange positions, half in the candlelight and half in shade, stood a little company of people I had never seen before.

Behind the table stood a noble lady in a rich silk domino of black and gold—it hid her hair and her figure, and only her eyes could be seen through her white satin mask with its fall of black lace. Who was she? The Donna Laura, perhaps? She did not speak or move.

Near her was a gallant gentleman, in black coat and breeches, and a gay-flowered cravat. He had a black mask, and a black cocked hat with a rosette. He must be Florindo, the handsome young lover of the puppet-troupe—if I had been Rosaura, and not a poor rascal of a Scaramouch, I would certainly have fallen in love with him.

Behind them, in a pink mask, on a divan, reclined a little Countess, richly attired.

On my right, nearest to the table of sweets and dainties, was a tiny Persian Princess . . . she alone, who was not so high as the table, wore no mask, and the candles lit up her fluff of golden curls, and her blue puzzled eyes and red pouting mouth.

And on my left, posed ready for the dance, was a small Coquette—a figure in a rose-pink crinoline, tight white bodice, rose-red velvet slippers, a high-dressed wig of rose-pink wool, and a mask of crimson satin.

Who were they all? The puppets stepped down from the wall? I looked at the wall, and there hung the puppets still, a limp, drooping company. Then who were these? And why did they not speak or move? True, I thought I heard the languid little Countess sigh, and I know I heard Florindo giggle—yet they all seemed under a spell. I must break it.

I banged my long rolling-pin on the floor, and hopped across it, and begged the pink Coquette to dance with me. She turned her head aside and burst out laughing.

"Why, you are Bridget!" I cried.

It was true! They were no dolls. The Donna Laura was Bridget's Mummy, the Persian Princess Nan, the lovely Countess Chloe, and the handsome young Florindo Ivy! We laughed and chattered and admired each other's dresses; and after the birthday tea of cakes and sweets, we danced the dances of all countries—Italian, French, and Russian, Spanish and English, and tore the streamers down, and wound each other in their nets.

A bell rang! Who could it be? Someone was at the door below. Florindo went to see. We heard great laughter, and Bridget cried, "It is my Milkman!"

Yes, it was the old Milkman who came every evening and chattered nonsense with us all. We all ran down to see him. He clapped his hands and capered when he saw us.

"*Brava! brava!* It is the Carnival!"

"You must dance with me!" cried Bridget.

She took his hand and pulled him up the stairs. In the long room the merry old peasant danced with the little pink Coquette, while I sang an Italian tune to keep them going.

It was a lovely party.

At bedtime the empty room was strewn with coloured streamers, tinsel rosettes, crumbs of cakes and sweets, and burnt-out coloured candles, with nobody to enjoy them but the puppets on the wall.

IV

ROSAURA'S BIRTHDAY

The charming Rosaura was nineteen years old, and she was not yet married. The loveliest creature in Siena, she led a gay and happy life. So gay and happy, indeed, that although she had many suitors, she would agree to marry none of them.

"Why should I?" said she. "While I am unwedded, I am free to dance where I will; but if I were wedded I should be chained to my hearth. I would have to make the minestrone, and cook the macaroni, for if you have a husband you must feed him. And what time would be left over for fun and laughter? No, while I am young I will dance. On the day I find my first grey hair, Florindo, I will take you for my husband."

Florindo was the handsomest of her suitors, and the one she liked the best. Messer Pantaleone was richer, but then he was wrinked with age. Brighella the Moor was more exciting, but they said he had a terrible temper. The learned Doctor Savio was wiser, but Rosaura could not understand half the long words he used. Now Florindo had attractive manners, a sweet temper, a sufficient fortune, and he was, in addition, nearly as young as Rosaura herself.

"Ah, it is beautiful to be young!" cried Rosaura; and she put on her mask and her domino, and went with Florindo to the Carnival. And late at night, when she had returned to bed, she heard the singers going through the street, and the rosy glow of their torchlight shone on her ceiling, and they paused under her window and sang the Song of Youth.

Later still, when they had passed by, came a single singer with his mandolin, and sang the love-song of Italy:

> "Flower of the Nut!
> Enjoy love and be happy,
> For life without love is worth nothing!"

"How true!" said Rosaura. "Tomorrow Florindo shall take me again to the Carnival. Now, if I was married, I should have to stay at home and cook the minestrone."

In vain the old Pantaleone shook his money-bags in her ear. In vain Brighella the Moor flourished his scimitar before her eyes. In vain the learned Doctor talked to her of love in Greek and Latin. Florindo alone did not urge her. He loved youth as she did. He did not want minestrone. As long as she would dance with him, he was happy. Time enough for marriage when the grey hair came.

So they went night after night to the Carnival; life was all paper flowers and gold tinsel, cakes and sweet drinks, masks and dominoes, torches and mandolins, singing and dancing, and coming home by starlight. One night Rosaura came home so late that it was morning, and at the door of her house she met the Milkman. She had never seen him before, although every day she drank milk without asking whence it came. For all she knew, it ran out of a tap in the wall. The Milkman was old and merry; he had brown withered hands, matted grey hair, a shabby coat, and very bright eyes. He greeted Rosaura.

"Good morning, pretty lady!"

"Good morning," said Rosaura. "Who are you?"

"I am the Milkman, my dear."

"Are you? What funny clothes you have for the Carnival!"

"These are not my Carnival clothes," said the old man. "No, indeed, pretty lady. These are the clothes I work in."

"Work? What is that?"

"It is what keeps you young when youth is gone—if it does not make you old before your time."

"I don't understand you," said Rosaura. "Dancing keeps *me* young."

"Why, so it does—when it does not wear you out entirely. Dancing and work together—that's what does it."

"But you are old!" cried Rosaura.

"I *look* old," said the Milkman, "and so, my dear, will you one day. When that day comes, may you dance as young as I do. But if you do nothing but dance till then, you will love it no longer, and then you will really and truly be old."

As he spoke, a party of belated singers came down the street, singing the Song of Youth; and the old Milkman caught Rosaura round the waist, and danced her as she had never been danced before.

But when he had departed, with his little mule and milk-cart, she ran into her house and sat down on the couch, and cried. The day looked in, and made the walls and windows golden, but still Rosaura cried. At midday, when Florindo arrived with a great bouquet of flowers, he found her in her rose-pink Carnival frock, with her black domino dropping round her feet, and her lace mask lying crumpled on the floor, sobbing her heart out on the elegant couch.

"Rosaura, weeping!" cried Florindo. "Ah, what has been done? Explain it! I will undo it. And who has done it? Name him! I will run him through the heart."

Rosaura lifted her head with its tumbled puffs and curls, and looked at him with her tear-stained eyes.

"Alas," said she, "there is nothing to do, and no one to run through. The truth is, I am afraid of growing old. I dance too much, and I work too little. In fact, I do not work at all; and I am not sure that I know what work is. Do you, Florindo?"

"I will not rest," said Florindo ardently, "until I have found out!"

"Thanks, dear Florindo. Do so! There is no time to be lost, for my birthday happens in four days from now and I shall turn twenty. Twenty! To think of it! I feel the grey hair coming at the word. Yes, I must set to work without delay." Rosaura rose, and shook out her crumpled frock. "What delicious flowers!" she said. "I will take them to the Carnival tonight. Call for me in good time."

During the day each of her suitors presented himself, and to each in turn Rosaura confided her trouble. And she let it be known that she would bestow her hand on whichever of her wooers could provide her with work to keep her young for ever. It seemed to them a strange notion, for each had his own idea of what work meant, and they could not imagine the charming creature applying herself to it. However, since it was her desire, she must be satisfied; and Pantaleone, spurred

by his first gleam of hope, promised her work the very next day. When Florindo came that night to escort her to the Carnival, he found her the joyous Rosaura of yesterday. He had to confess:

"I have not yet discovered what work is."

"No matter," said Rosaura; "Messer Pataleone knows. He is going to show me tomorrow. Let us dance."

The following morning she presented herself betimes at Pantaleone's house. The old man led her at once to the kitchen where his servants were.

"Look," said he, "these people work for me all day long. But one of the maids was married a week ago, and you shall take her place. I leave you in the hands of my housekeeper, who will tell you what to do."

When they were alone, the housekeeper looked Rosaura up and down with disapproval. "You can never work in a silk frock, with flowers in your hair," said she. "Put on this cotton apron and tie up your head in a handkerchief."

Rosaura obeyed. Then she was given a broom and a brush, and told to sweep and scrub. Then she had to clean the stove, and prepare the vegetables, and polish the gold and silver plate, and make the beds, and set the table, and wash up the dishes, and turn the spit, and work the churn, and mend the linen, and knead the bread, and do twenty other things besides. As she did all these things very badly, by the end of the day her arms and feet and back ached so much that she was ready to drop.

The old Pantaleone came to her wreathed in

smiles. "Well, my charmer," said he, "have I not gained the prize? When you are married to me,

you will be able to work like this from week's end to week's end, and keep as young as you are today."

But Rosaura stamped her poor tired foot at him. "I never felt so old in all my life!" she cried; and she slapped his face and ran home as fast as her weary limbs would carry her. There she found Florindo waiting, eager to take her to the dance. But, "Dance!" sighed she. "I feel I never want to dance again." And she went straight to bed.

The next day Brighella the Moor came to her and said, "Beautiful Rosaura! This is a strange whim of yours. But if it is work you want, I have plenty to offer you."

"Anything," said Rosaura, "so long as it will keep me young, and is not scrubbing floors and pots."

"It has to do with nobler things than pots," said Brighella. "Yesterday my stable-boy ran away. You shall take his place, and tend my Arab steeds."

He led her to his stables full of the finest horses from Arabia, and handing her a comb of steel said, "Curry their coats!" and left her.

There were fifty horses in the stables, each more mettlesome than the last. The first whisked his tail at her, the second whinnied at her, the third rolled his eyes at her, the fourth kicked his heel at her, the fifth snorted fire at her, and so it went on. At the end of the day she had not dared to touch one of their coats, and when Brighella came to her he found her crouching in a corner of the stable, her teeth chattering with fright.

"Well, my beauty," cried the Moor, "is the prize mine? When you are my bride, you shall curry my steeds all day long, and never grow old!"

"Ah me!" wailed Rosaura. "Shall I ever feel young again?" She threw the curry-comb in Brighella's face, and ran home as though wild horses were after her. Florindo was on her doorstep, waiting to lead her to the dance. But, "Dance," cried she, "when I am shaking with terror in every limb? Ah, Florindo, I have lost all heart for dancing!" And she threw herself on her bed and slept, without undressing.

On the third day, the day before her birthday, the learned Doctor presented himself, saying, "Superlative Rosaura! Is it true that you would preserve your juvenescence by operose means?"

"What does *that* mean?" asked Rosaura. "If you mean, do I want work that will keep me young, yes, I do. But first, have you any horses?"

"I abominate the quadrupeds!" replied the learned Doctor.

"And shall I have to sweep your rooms?"

"On no account!" replied the learned Doctor. "In my house sweeping and dusting are expressly forbidden. They would disturb my books and papers."

Rosaura accompanied him to his rooms, which

were so deep in dust that she sneezed as soon as she put her nose inside the door. The learned Doctor seated her at a big table littered with papers, gave her a ream of foolscap, a pint of ink, twelve quill pens, and an old encyclopaedia in a hundred volumes. Bidding her copy out everything she could find in these books relating to the Assyrians, he left her till evening. He then returned, beaming at her from behind his spectacles.

"Well, my child, and have your labours refreshed your spirit?" he asked. "And will you become my helpmate and my secretary to the end of your days?"

"Refreshed indeed!" said Rosaura wearily. "I have such a headache that I can hardly think!"

And pushing books, pens, ink and paper off the table with a sweep of her arm, she hurried to her own house; where, as usual, Florindo was before her, dressed for the dance. But, "I cannot hold my head up," she sighed; "it is splitting, Florindo!" And instead of dancing she laid her aching head upon the pillow and fell asleep.

The following day was her birthday, and the great Day of the Carnival. Rosaura awoke and found herself surrounded by handsome presents: from Pantaleone a golden bracelet, from Brighella

an Arab pony, from the learned Doctor a Latin dictionary bound in calfskin, and from Florindo a basket of flowers, in which was hidden a charming pair of high-heeled slippers. There was also a queer little wooden cow, with loosely jointed legs, that danced when it was dangled. Where that came from, nobody knew.

When Florindo arrived a little later, he found Rosaura practising steps in her new shoes. "Dear Florindo!" she cried. "I have just turned twenty! Do I look very old? Have you yet found out the work to keep me young?"

"Alas," said he, "not yet. And you scarcely look a day older."

She gave him her hand to kiss. "Well, after all, it is my birthday," she said, "so perhaps I need not work for once. How can I thank you for these exquisite slippers?"

"Come and dance in them," he answered. "The Carnival will soon be in full fling."

Off they went together, the charming Rosaura and the handsome young Florindo, and danced from noon till night and from night till morning. They danced as though they would never tire, in the great open place in the heart of Siena, where people big and little in masks and dominoes danced too. The merrymakers threw coloured streamers and tinsel flowers, munched almond and raisin cake, ate whipped cream with a spoon, and drank sweet drinks in which they toasted Rosaura on her birthday.

Day was breaking when she danced back to her house, led by Florindo, escorted by all her suitors, and followed by the throng of maskers: a King, a Queen, Harlequin, Columbine, Scaramouch, Punchinello, and all the rest. There at the door stood the merry old Milkman with his little mule-cart.

"Good morning, pretty lady," said he.

"Good morning, Milkman," said Rosaura.

"And have you had a happy birthday at the Carnival, my dear?"

"The happiest of my life," cried Rosaura. "Would it could last for ever! But I have turned twenty, and I am growing old already."

"Have you tried work?" asked the Milkman.

"Yes, till I dropped, and was frightened, and my head ached, and I lost all heart for dancing."

"Then you overdid it," said the Milkman. "And how do you feel now, after dancing all night long?"

"As fresh as a daisy," said Rosaura.

"Then that's the work for you," said the old man.

Rosaura was overjoyed. "Florindo, do you hear?" cried she. "Dancing also is work!"

"Yes, yes," said the Milkman, "there's no work so hard as dancing, if you don't know when you've had enough."

"I could never have enough!" cried Rosaura. "Florindo without knowing it has discovered the work for me. I wish to dance with Florindo for ever and ever, and never be tired, and always be as young as I am now."

"Perhaps it can be managed," said the Milkman. "Fetch me the little wooden cow I left at your door this morning, and bring also a cup."

Rosaura ran for the cow and a cup, and when she had brought them the Milkman milked the cow into the cup. The milk of the wooden cow ran down like sawdust. When the cup was full to the brim the Milkman said:

"Now you can have your wish, my dear. For whoever sips of this cup will remain what he is for ever and ever. But think twice before you sip."

"Once is enough!" cried Rosaura. "Who would not remain for ever young and pretty and happy if she had the chance? And wear a silk dress, and high-heeled shoes, and dance without growing tired?"

And she sipped the cup of sawdust. Then Florindo cried, "Hand me the cup, Rosaura, that I too may always be young and handsome, and never too tired to dance with you!"

And he too sipped. Then Pantaleone cried, "Hand *me* the cup that I may always keep my money-bags, and dance in the Carnival!"

"And me," cried the Doctor, "that I may always keep my learning, and dance in the Carnival!"

"And me," cried Brighella, "that I may always be strong and bold, and dance in the Carnival!"

"And me!—And me!—And me!" cried one and another: King and Harlequin, Queen and Columbine, all wished to go on dancing in the Carnival for ever. So one by one they sipped the sawdust of the jointed cow, until there was none left. While they sipped the old Milkman chuckled, and when the cup was empty he cried:

"Now dance, pretty lady! Dance with me! Dance, all the Carnival, dance, and never grow tired!"

He caught Rosaura's hands and danced her through Siena, followed by her suitors and all the Carnival train. And as they danced they grew smaller and smaller and smaller, and their limbs turned to wood and their joints to wires. And when at last the Milkman stopped, they all fell down in a heap, and Rosaura hung in his hands as limp as a doll—which in fact she was.

The Milkman held her up for a moment between his finger and thumb, and, "There, pretty lady, you have your wish!" said he. "Though you live to a hundred you shall not lose your young face, and though you dance all day long you shall never grow tired." He gathered up the little puppets in his hands, the old Pantaleone, the dark-skinned Brighella, the spectacled Doctor, the handsome Florindo, the charming Rosaura, and all the rest; and he piled them on his milk-cart and wheeled them away.

V

ANINA

Our house was not quite at the top of the hill. The road wound up above us for a little, and then stopped in the market-place on the hilltop, where the old men and women sat selling things under big bright umbrellas. All round the market square were funny little shops, where you could buy drinks and sweetmeats and little cakes, and beautiful coloured paper, and dolls' pots and bowls, and queer cheeses, and funny sausages, and strange fruits, and golden oil, and red and white wine in bottles with long necks and round bodies all dressed up in straw—and, of course, Pasta.

I must tell you now what Pasta is. The thick macaroni like long pipes is Pasta; and the thin vermicelli like tangled hair is Pasta; and the little stars and letters which, if you are lucky, the cook sometimes puts in your soup—they too are Pasta. Just as bread can be of many sorts: white bread or brown bread, cottage loaves or tin loaves, breakfast rolls or crescents: so Pasta is of many sorts, far more than you have ever seen. And just as bread is important to English people, so Pasta is important to Italians. It is made of flour paste of all shapes and sizes. Besides the macaroni, the vermicelli, the stars and the letters, there are:

Shells and
Bells and
Nuts and
Apple-pips and
Needle-points and
Fleas' Eyes and

Horses' Teeth and
Holy Seeds and
Olive Stones and
Linen Sheets and
Hearts and
Diamonds and
Feathers and
The Virgin's Tears—

all made out of flour and water, to be eaten in soup, or covered with tomato sauce, or sprinkled with cheese. There are other kinds as well, but these will do for the present; and to all the kinds the Italians have given funny names or pretty ones. What we call vermicelli, they call Angels' hair.

All the things they sold in the little shops in that market-place on the hilltop were brought up from Florence, miles away, in carts drawn by white oxen. The oxen were as white as milk or marble, and drew the carts in teams side by side. Their wide horns were adorned with red tassels, and so were their tails. They had collars of little bells, which rang like silver and shone like gold. When the beautiful oxen appeared in the village with their cartloads of red wine and white, and oil, and fruit, and cheeses, and sausages, and sweetmeats, the most important thing they brought was the Pasta.

One day Anina, our cook, came to us with a dark face, shaking her head. Anina did not live with us. She had a little house in the village, and a husband and some children of her own. But every morning she came and worked in the kitchen, and cooked the Pasta for dinner; because of course in Italy we had Pasta like everyone else. But on this day Anina looked unhappy, because there was no Pasta in the village.

"Why not, Anina?"

"It has not come. They have none in the city to send up to us."

"Never mind, Anina. Perhaps it will come tomorrow."

But it did not come tomorrow—or the next day—or the next. Everybody in the village was unhappy. How could they live without their Pasta? Bread and potatoes are not the same thing at all. Nothing can take the place of Pasta. It was a black week in Fiesole when the Pasta did not come from Florence.

Then one morning Anina came running in with a shining face, crying:

"Good news! Good news!"

"What is it, Anina?"

"The King of Tripoli has come!"

"The King of Tripoli? Are you certain, Anina?" Bridget's Mummy looked at me, and I looked at

Bridget's Mummy. We did not know that there *was* a King of Tripoli.

"But yes, I am certain! The King of Tripoli has come to Italy, and has brought the Pasta with him. Tomorrow they will send it up from Florence."

That was all Anina could tell us. It did not sound very likely, but she was sure it was so. That morning she sang at her work, in her deep rough voice. And the next day the grand white oxen with their scarlet tassels climbed the steep hill to the market-place, ringing their golden bells. And when they heard the bells ringing, out of their shops and houses ran all the men and women and children, to cheer and laugh and cry, "The Pasta has come! The Pasta has come! The King of Tripoli has sent the Pasta!"

It was perfectly true; the oxen-carts were laden with Pasta of all sorts.

But the funny thing *is*, that there *isn't* a King of Tripoli; there isn't, really.

VI

THE KING OF TRIPOLI BRINGS THE PASTA

It came to pass one year that the corn crops failed, and there was no flour in Italy. Such a disaster had never been known before. The people lived as long as they could on the Pasta in their cupboards. Then they went to the shops for last year's flour, to take home and make into more Pasta. The grocers sold the flour as though it were gold-dust. At last there was no more flour to buy or sell, and the day dawned on which all Italy sat down to dinner without Pasta.

Such a wail went up from the throats of the people that it was heard across the sea. King Nero of Tripoli heard it where he sat on his jewelled throne, and he lifted his head to listen.

"What is that?" asked the King of Tripoli.

"It is the mosquitoes humming in the marshes," said his Minister.

The next day, at the same hour, the wail was heard again, a little louder; and again the King of Tripoli asked, "What is that?"

His Minister answered, "It is the Pilgrims singing in the desert."

On the third day the same thing happened, but now the wail seemed nearer still. Once more the King asked, "What is that?" and his Minister answered, "It is the sea breaking on the shore."

On the fourth day the wail was so loud that it seemed to arise in Tripoli itself. "What is that?"

"It is the wind howling in the streets."

On the fifth day the wail seemed to come from the palace gates. "What is that?"

"It is the lions roaring in the garden."

The sixth day the wail seemed to be over the King's very head. "My Minister, what is that?"

"O King, it is the cracking of God's thunder!"

But the seventh day the wail rang in the King of Tripoli's heart. It could get no closer than that, and he knew it was the cry of pain, and fear, and hunger. He did not ask again, "What is that?" but arose and said, "It is the crying of men and children. Order my boat to make ready."

"For what reason, O King?" asked his Minister.

"For none but this—that I cannot rest until I know why the children cry."

So the Golden Galley of Tripoli set sail, with the King upon it; and following the cry across the sea, he came to Italy. Here on the seashore he saw many people; some sat and wrung their hands, others ran about and tore their hair, and all were wailing with the sound he had heard in his heart.

"For what do you cry?" asked the King of Tripoli.

"For Pasta."

The King of Tripoli mounted his golden car, drawn by the Royal Oxen, and went further inland. Along all the roads the people stood and wailed.

"What do you want?" the King asked them.

"Pasta! Pasta!"

Then he came to the villages and the cities, and wherever he went he heard and saw the same thing; and whenever he put his question, the answer was always, "Pasta! We have no Pasta!"

The King of Tripoli had a heart like a child, and he could not bear it. In a village set high on a hilltop the children crowded round his golden car and held out their hands, imploring, "A little Pasta! Throw us a little Pasta, please!" He stopped his oxen and leaned out of his car to address a lovely child with a fair skin and red-gold hair. "Why have you no Pasta, pretty child?" asked the King of Tripoli.

She looked in his face, turned as red as the setting sun, burst into tears, and ran away. The children called after her, "Bianca! Bianca!" but she would not come out of hiding.

"I have frightened her," thought the King of Tripoli sadly. However, the other children did not seem to fear him; therefore he asked again, "Why is there no Pasta in Italy?"

"The flour crop failed, Your Majesty," said one.

"How came it to fail?"

"Nobody knows. Our mothers think the crops were cursed," said another, "yet nobody could see the blight."

"We have eaten all the Pasta up, and can make no more," said a third.

"We are hungry!" cried the children, all together; and one and another pleaded for his special favourite dish. "Oh, how I would like a plateful of shells!"

"The little bells are nicer!" "Needle-points for me!" "*I* like the Holy Seeds!" "Feathers! Feathers!" "Olive-stones!" "Nuts and Apple-pips!" "Hearts and Diamonds!" "Horses' Teeth—delicious!" "Fleas' Eyes are better!" "Give *me* the White Linen!" "I'd rather have the Stars!" "Oh, no! The Angels' hair!" "I want the Virgin's Tears!" And then again, all together, "We are hungry!"

The King of Tripoli put his hands to his head. "If you cry you will break poor Nero's heart," he said. "Be good children now, and I will try to bring you your Pasta."

At this the children cheered and laughed for the first time for weeks, and ran eagerly to tell their mothers, leaving King Nero thinking. He always found thinking a hard job, especially in Italian, which was not his own tongue. He did not really know what Pasta was, but he had heard some words he understood.

So first he went down to the seashore and cried aloud, "O Sea, give me your shells, for the children are hungry!"

"With pleasure," said the Sea, "if the Church will give you its bells."

The King of Tripoli went at once to the Church and begged, "O Church, give me your bells!"

"Gladly," said the Church, "if the Bushes will give you their nuts."

"Dear Bushes," cried the King of Tripoli, "will you give me your nuts?"

"Of course we will," said the Bushes, "when the Apples give you their pips."

"Spare me your pips, Apples," pleaded the King.

"As soon," said the Apples, "as the Olives give you their stones."

"O Olives, give me your stones!"

"Willingly—when the Birds give you their feathers!"

"Flying Birds, give me your feathers!"

"By all means, when the Fleas give you their eyes!"

"Little Fleas, give me your eyes!"

"Certainly, when the Horses give you their teeth!"

"Most noble Horses, give me your teeth!"

"With happiness—when the Laundresses give you their linen!"

"You handsome Laundresses, will you not give me your linen!"

"Take it—when the Seamstresses have given you their needle-points."

"Nimble Seamstresses, give me your needle-points!"

"Yes, yes, when the Queen has given you her diamonds!"

The King of Tripoli hastened to Rome, and there he sought audience of the Queen. She received him in her throne-room, and came to meet him, sparkling with diamonds.

"What brings you here?" she asked.

"Queen of Italy, give me your diamonds!"

"Why?"

"Because the people are hungry."

"You shall have my diamonds," said the Queen, "when the people have given you their hearts."

The King went forth into the streets and cried, "Beloved People! Give me your hearts!"

"Yes," said the People, "when the Sky gives you its stars."

"Ah, Sky! Give me your stars!"

"They are yours, when the Angels give you their hair."

"White Angels! Give me your hair!"

"Joyfully, when the Saints give you the Holy Seeds!"

"Shining Saints! Give me the Holy Seeds!"

"You shall have them all, when the Virgin gives you her tears."

"Mother Mary! Give me your tears, for the children of the earth are hungry." And the King of Tripoli knelt at the Virgin's feet.

"Alas!" said the Virgin. "I need my tears to weep with."

"Nay, but why?"

"Because I saw a fair-skinned child mock at a little black one," said the Virgin.

"Never mind," said the King of Tripoli, "she knew no better."

"Ah," said the Virgin, "but Earth, who sees no difference between black and white, is angry with the fair child, and refuses to bear corn in her country, until of her own free will she kisses a black man."

"But while the Earth is angry," said the King of Tripoli, "the child goes hungry. So for your Child's sake give me your tears, and if needs be I will weep in your stead." And indeed, as he spoke the black face of the King of Tripoli was as wet with tears as the Virgin's own. When she saw this the Virgin stooped and kissed his forehead, and said, "Here are my tears."

He put them in a golden jar, and set it in the front of his chariot. Then he drove his White Oxen back the way he had come, and the Saints gave him the Holy Seeds, and the Angels gave him their hair, and the Sky gave him its stars, and the People gave him their hearts, and the Queen her diamonds, and the Seamstresses their needle-points, and the Laundresses their linen, and the Horses their teeth, and the Fleas their eyes, the Birds their feathers, the Olives their stones, the Apples their pips, the Bushes their nuts, the Church its bells, and the Sea its shells. You never saw such a load of things as was piled on the King of Tripoli's golden car.

Then what a Royal Progress he made through Italy! He drove his White Oxen from end to end, through all the cities and villages on plain and hilltop, and to all the lonely huts that stood by themselves. Wherever he went he scattered his largess on either side, in great handfuls, and wherever it fell it turned to Pasta; whether it were bells or shells, pips or nuts, Holy Seeds or Angels' hair, it made no difference—all became Pasta.

And wherever he went the people ran after him, laughing and shouting, "The King of Tripoli has brought the Pasta! The King of Tripoli has brought the Pasta!"

At last he reached the village on the hilltop where he had spoken with the children, and everybody was lined up to meet him in the market-place, for the tale of his kindness and bounty had travelled before him, and even those who had not seen him loved him. As his White Oxen entered the market square, little Bianca ran out of the crowd. She sprang into his golden car, threw her arms around his neck, and pressing her fair cheek to his black one, she gave him a kiss. "I am sorry I mocked the little black boy," she said.

The King of Tripoli beamed with happiness as he put the golden jar into her hands. "This is for you," he said; and when she opened it, it was full of the Virgin's tears, turned into the finest Pasta, like all the rest.

Side by side they drove around the market square scattering the Pasta like manna as they went. And the people set up a mighty cheer, and clapped their hands, and cried,

"The King of Tripoli has brought the Pasta! Huzza! The King of Tripoli has brought the Pasta!"

But best of all, the Earth, at the same moment, began to grow corn.

VII

NAN AND CECCHINO

Nan, Bridget and Chloe's little sister, was fair even for an English child. To the Italians, who called her Nanina and adored her, she must have seemed as fair as an angel. She had a wonderful mop of white-gold hair, and a skin as white as the tops of the Carrara Mountains which we could see gleaming in the distance like snow: but they were not covered with snow, they were white because they were made of pure marble. Nan's blue eyes and the pink in her cheeks only made her white skin whiter. She was tiny and light, and played in a world of her own.

We noticed when we went out with her that she was afraid of the animals she met, and especially of big dogs. So her Mummy thought it would be a good plan to get a very little puppy to live in the house, hoping that Nan would look on the little creature as a sort of toy, and so get used to it by the time it was a dog; and in time get used to all dogs.

Halfway down the hill to Florence was a beautiful old Villa falling into ruins; it was called the Canovaia, and Bridget and Chloe and Nan had lived there once, before they came up to Fiesole. When the owners of the beautiful house went away, they left the servants there to attend to Bridget's Mummy and her children; and these servants, and their big family, still lived there. They had many animals and fowls living there with them, and among them a dog who had had puppies. So one day we went down to the Canovaia to choose a puppy, and we chose for our tiny white Nan a tiny white puppy called Cecchino.

In all Italy I never saw a house so romantic as the Canovaia. It was like a beautiful old picture that is peeling and fading. It stood in a lane behind a high wall, but its terraced garden lay behind it on the hillside, open to the sunlight. There was a great dim square court with a fountain, stone benches, flowering trees in tubs, and a staircase leading to a deep shady balcony hung with vines. This again led into the upstairs rooms, and one had a turret looking out over Florence. Downstairs the chief rooms ran along in a suite at the back of the house, overlooking the garden; the rooms were silent and muffled, with old-fashioned chairs and mirrors, tables and couches, cabinets and shelves of unopened books, all unused and growing musty together. Behind these rooms were the big gaunt kitchens and living-rooms of the servants; they were spacious and full of litter: children and pots, chickens and vegetables, puppies and cats and goats seemed to be everywhere. They had spread into the courtyard, and you felt that in a very little while, if the owners did not return, they would spread into the empty salons; where the chickens would lay their eggs on the couches, and go to roost on the cabinets. The woman made us some chocolate, and we drank it on the terrace above the garden, which was full of persimmon-trees, roses, and violets; weeds and flowers rambled everywhere in the February sunlight. The Canovaia, inside and out, might have been the palace of the Sleeping Princess.

Before we left we arranged for the man to bring Cecchino on a certain day; and we took away with us a basketful of the gold-red persimmons. The children loved them.

The day came, and Cecchino with it. We waited anxiously to see how Nan would take to her new toy. But Nan did not take to him at all, nor Cecchino to Nan. Scream after scream filled the house at the first sight of him, and yap after yap was added to the screams. Cecchino was hurriedly removed, but Nan was still screaming when the old Milkman came to the door. He heard her, and asked, "Why is the Bambina crying?"

"She is afraid of the little dog," we told him.

"She has fear, eh? But you can cure her fear."

"How?"

"There is a certain herb which cures all fear. You must procure some of it, steep it in boiling water, and bathe the child in the infusion three nights running. Then she will have no more fear."

The old man left the milk, and went away. But in a short while there was a loud knocking on the door, and there he was again, his hands full of leaves. "*Ecco!*" he said. "Here is the Herb of Fear."

"But will it really cure her?"

He shrugged. "Ask Anina, if you do not believe me. She will tell you the same as I."

Next day, when she came, we did ask Anina.

"Yes," she said, "that is the Herb of Fear. If you

have had a shock or a fright, you have only to wash your hands in the herb-water, and the fear will go."

This happened a day or two before I left Italy. Nan had not been bathed with the herb when I departed. I do not think she ever was. But she grew fond of Cecchino, and she no longer fears dogs; so perhaps Anina bathed her in secret. Who knows?

VIII

THE HERB OF FEAR

One morning the Man of Carrara sat in his Marble Mountain making things. By the end of the day he had made a child and a puppy, both out of pure white marble. He called the child Nanina and the puppy Cecchino. When he had put the last stroke to them, he sent them away to be filled with life, and set about making something else.

As soon as the spark of life had been lit in them, Cecchino cried, "Nanina!" and Nanina cried, "Cecchino!" and Cecchino leaped into Nanina's arms, and Nanina cuddled and kissed him. They recognized each other instantly, for were they not made of the same stuff? However, they had not much time for cuddles and kisses. Nanina was sent one way and Cecchino another, to find their homes on earth.

In due course Nanina came to live in Fiesole on the hilltop, with a garden that looked over the whole world. And Cecchino found a lodging in an old house that was falling into decay, but was a very pleasant place for a little dog to make mischief in. For it had great empty rooms full of silk hangings and tassels, and a big wild garden full of roses and persimmons.

Nanina was happy on her hilltop, and the only thing that cast a shadow on her days was her fear of Monsters. There were so many Monsters in the world—Monsters with horns, Monsters with swishing tails, Monsters with green eyes, Monsters with yapping voices; and all of them had four legs instead of two, like reasonable people. Of people Nanina had no fear whatever.

Cecchino for his part feared nothing on four legs. He would have worried a herd of elephants as gaily as he worried the silk fringe on the rich faded curtains in his dwelling. But he *was* afraid of Giantesses. If ever he heard of a Giantess anywhere near he ran and hid under a couch, and would not come out till the danger was past. He roamed at will wherever he pleased, and every day he ran down to Florence to drink of the green Arno, which tasted better than any water in Italy. But he never on any account ran up to Fiesole, because he had heard that a Giantess lived there.

One day news came that all the Brigands in Italy were on the way, and nobody was safe. Everybody got the shivers and shakes. When Nanina went for a walk that morning she found all the shops and houses shut and bolted. This vexed her, because she wanted a persimmon to eat after dinner, and she had two soldi to buy it with. She ran all round the market square rattling at the doors, while the people ran into their cupboards and got under their beds, quite sure that the Brigands were after them. Then Nanina got cross, for when she wanted a persimmon she *wanted* a persimmon. As she stood in the empty market square, wondering what to do, she saw the old Milkman coming down one of the twisty streets with his milk-cart behind him, and a sprig in his hat. Brigands or no Brigands, the milk must be left.

He knew Nanina well, and stopped at once to ask, "What is the matter, Nanina?"

"I want a persimmon."

"There are no persimmons."

"Why?"

"The Brigands have taken them all."

"But I *want* one!"

"Then you must go to the Brigands," said the Milkman.

"Then I will!" said Nanina. And off she went.

Over the mountains she saw the Brigands coming from their lair, streams and streams of them, in black slouch hats and big cloaks. The people were flying before them in all directions, and the Brigand Chief was shouting, "Ha, ha! Ha, ha!" as he always did when he saw people flying before him. The

crowd was so great that Nanina could hardly push through it. But she waved her little hands, and stamped her little feet, and her white cheeks flushed, and her blue eyes flashed, and her bright hair glittered in the sun as she cried, "Out of my way! I want to see the Brigand Chief!"

"Run, child, run!" the people cried. "The Brigand Chief will gobble you up as soon as look at you!"

"Stuff and nonsense!" said Nanina. "Out of my way *at once*!"

And through the flying crowd she marched, till she met the Brigand Chief face to face. For the first time in his life he saw himself confronted by sparkling blue eyes, blowing gold hair, two pink cheeks, two little feet that stamped at him, two little fists that shook at him, and an angry little voice that cried:

"How *dare* you take all the persimmons in Italy, when I want one after dinner? Give me a persimmon this instant, or I'll tell on you!"

The Brigand Chief turned pale. "You wouldn't do that, would you?" he said.

"Yes, I *would*!" said Nanina fiercely. "Give me a persimmon *at once*!"

The Brigand Chief shook in his shoes. "Alas!" he whispered, "we have eaten them all!" and he burst into tears. Seeing their Chief weep, all the other Brigands confessed, "Alas, alas, it is true! We have eaten them." And they also burst into tears.

"Very well," said Nanina, "I shall go and tell."

"Wait!" cried the Chief. "There is one hope left. In an old wilderness of a garden on the way to Florence grows the finest persimmon-tree in Italy. That tree alone we have not robbed. Because—"

"Because?" demanded Nanina.

"Because," said the Brigand Chief in a low voice, "it is guarded by a Monster!" Then he threw up his hands to heaven, turned on his heel, and ran back as fast as he could to his lair, and never came out again; and all his Brigands followed him. So Italy was delivered for ever from Brigands by Nanina, in a single moment.

Everybody came and praised and petted her, but she was in such a temper that she would not listen to them. All she said was, "I want a persimmon! I want a persimmon to eat after dinner."

"You must wait till next year, little darling," said the people. "Next year when the persimmons are ripe, you shall eat them all."

"I don't want them all, *then*," said Nanina; "I want just one, *now*."

"But there are none now. The Brigands took them all."

"No, they didn't. They didn't take the tree in the old garden on the way to Florence. But—"

"But what, little darling?"

"It is guarded by a Monster," said Nanina tremulously. Her little lip quivered, and she began to sob.

At this moment the old Milkman pushed his way through the crowd. "What's the matter here?" he asked, and listened while one and another told him the story. Nanina herself was sobbing too hard to speak.

"It appears to me," said the Milkman at last, "that as Nanina has delivered you from Brigands, you ought to go and get her a persimmon."

But the people said, "We don't like Monsters," and turned on their heels and ran away as fast as they could to their homes, where they locked themselves in again.

Then the Milkman said to Nanina, "It appears to me that if you want a persimmon you must get it yourself."

"But *I* don't like Monsters either," sobbed Nanina.

"Well, well, that can be remedied. Do you see this sprig in my hat? It is called the Herb of Fear, not because it makes you afraid, but because it draws all the fear out of you. Listen carefully, Nanina, follow my counsel, and all will be well. I happen to know that this is the hour when the Monster you speak of goes down to Florence to drink the green

Arno. Now is your moment to go to the deserted garden, in the courtyard of which stands a ruined fountain. Throw this herb into the water, bathe yourself therein, and when you come out you will fear Monsters as little as you do Brigands."

The old man looked so wise and kind that Nanina trusted him. Off she ran as fast as she could, to reach the fountain before the Monster returned. She flung the Herb of Fear into the water and stripped off her frock; and just then—oh horror!—she heard the shrill voice of the Monster yapping at the gate. As quick as thought she jumped into the fountain. She had hardly done so when the Monster himself leaped over the wall and jumped in after her. For he had met the old Milkman at the gate, who had told him that the Giantess from Fiesole had come down to look for him; and his only chance was to bathe in the fountain and grow bold.

For a moment or two the courtyard was filled with splashes and cries and yelps. Then Nanina sat up on *her* side of the fountain shaking the water out of her curls, and the Monster sat up on *his* side shaking the water out of his coat. As soon as they set eyes on each other—

"Cecchino!" cried Nanina.

"Nanina!" cried Cecchino.

And Cecchino leaped into Nanina's arms, and Nanina cuddled and kissed him. They knew each other instantly, for were they not made of the same stuff?

Down in the garden the Monster and the Giantess went together, and soon a puppy and a little girl were eating persimmons to their hearts' conteut.

IX

NELLA'S DANCING SHOES

This was a Choosing Story. Sometimes when I have told stories to Bridget and Chloe and Nan all day long, and really can't think any more, I say, "Choose what shall be in the story."

Then everybody who is in the room chooses something.

BRIDGET: I choose a pair of Red Velvet Dancing Slippers. (Bridget has a pair of red velvet dancing slippers.)

CHLOE: I choose an Eagle.

THEIR MUMMY: I choose a Jungle.

ELEANOR: And I choose a Fan. Now wait a minute while I think.

When I have thought, which mustn't be more than a minute, the story begins, and goes on by itself.

Once upon a time there was a beautiful Dancer who lived in a garden in Italy.

BRIDGET: What was she called?

ELEANOR: She was called Nella.

BRIDGET: Oh. (Bridget's prettiest doll is called Nella.)

Nella was the loveliest dancer in the world, and all the people wanted her to come and dance at their parties. In the evening she would go down to Florence to their long salons hung with blue satin embroidered with flowers, or red velvet printed with gold, and dance on the polished floors under

twelve enormous chandeliers glittering with lights and lustres, which hung down like long diamond ear-drops in a Queen's ears; or else she would dance in their gardens on the lawns among the statues and roses and fountains, where all the trees were hung with lights like coloured stars. And whenever she danced in her rose-red velvet dancing slippers, all the people clapped their hands and shouted, "*Brava,* Nella! *Brava! Brava!*"

In Nella's cupboard at home were rows and rows of other slippers, of gold, and glass, and silk, and leather; but she never wore any of them when she went to dance for the people. For the rose-red velvet slippers were magic slippers which made her dance better than anyone else in Italy; and when she wore her other slippers, she couldn't dance at all. Nobody knew this but Nella.

One day Nella was in her garden picking roses, and because the dew was on the grass she had taken off her red velvet slippers and left them by her chair. Suddenly a great Eagle swooped out of the sky, caught the slippers in his beak, and flew away as swiftly as he had come. Nella gave a scream and stood on tiptoe, and reached out her arms, trying to touch the sky. But it was no good; the slippers and the Eagle had vanished entirely.

Then Nella sat down and cried and cried. She was to dance that night for the Prince of Florence, but when the people came to fetch her she was still sitting crying in the garden, and she wouldn't tell them why. She only sobbed, and said she wouldn't dance. They entreated in vain—no! she wouldn't dance. She couldn't, of course, because she had lost her magic slippers. Every day after that she sat in the garden watching the sky, and every night the people were sad because Nella, their beautiful dancer, would dance for them no more.

One day as Nella sat watching the sky for the Eagle she saw a rush of wings overhead. It was not the Eagle, however, but a flight of Swallows.

"Oh, Swallows!" cried Nella. "You go about in the sky as people go about on earth, so have you seen the great Eagle who stole my red velvet slippers?"

But the Swallows had never seen or heard of him, and flew away, and Nella wept.

The next day as she was watching, a flock of Wild Swans flew over her head.

"Oh, Swans!" cried Nella. "You go over more places in a year than most men travel in a lifetime, so have you seen the great Eagle who stole my red velvet slippers?"

But the Swans could give her no news of him, and *they* flew away, and Nella wept.

The next day as she was watching, she saw a thousand Starlings twinkle like stars over her garden.

"Oh, Starlings!" cried Nella. "You have been everywhere among the clouds, so have you in your travels ever met the great Eagle who stole my red velvet slippers?"

But the Starlings could tell her no more than the Swans and the Swallows, and they also flew away, and Nella wept.

On the fourth day as she sat in her garden a single shadow fluttered on the grass, and looking up she saw that it was made by a green Parrot with one red feather in his tail.

"Oh, Parrot!" cried Nella. "You live in strange countries and have seen many things, so have you seen the great Eagle who stole my red velvet slippers?"

"Certainly I have," said the Parrot.

"Oh, where?" cried Nella.

"I was sitting on a coconut-tree in a Jungle," said the Parrot, "and the Eagle flew over my head with your slippers in his beak. When he reached the very middle of the Jungle, he opened his beak and dropped the slippers, and that was the last I saw of him or them."

"Oh, Parrot!" cried Nella. "Where is the Jungle?"

"In the very middle of India," said the Parrot, and flew away.

Then Nella began to weep again, for it seemed

to her that her precious slippers might as well be in the Eagle's beak as in the middle of India, for all the use they were to her.

Just then she heard a voice say, "Come, come, I wouldn't cry if I were you!" and looking up she saw the Fan-Man looking through the gate. He was long and thin and dressed in green, and he had a green paper fan in his hand.

"What *would* you do, then?" said Nella. "The Eagle has dropped my red slippers in the very middle of the Jungle in the very middle of India, so there's nothing to do but cry. If I had wings like an Eagle or a Swallow or a Swan or a Starling or a Parrot, I wouldn't need to cry."

"Tush, tush!" said the Fan-Man. "There are more ways of flying than with wings."

Then he came into the garden and told Nella to stand on tiptoe as though she were going to dance, and when she was on the very points of her toes he opened his fan and fanned her. Up she went into the air like a bird, and after her went the Fan-Man, fanning with all his might. He fanned her right across Italy and Turkey and Persia until they reached India; and when he had fanned her to the very middle of the Jungle, the Fan-Man stopped, and Nella dropped.

Now in the very middle of the Jungle in the very middle of India there is a Blue Pool, so Nella dropped into the Pool and went down and down and down till she got to the bottom. At the bottom of the Pool she found the Blue Nymph of the Pool sitting on a lotus leaf, and to Nella's great joy the Nymph had the red velvet slippers on. But as she had never seen slippers before, and hadn't the least idea what they were for, instead of having them on her feet she had hung them in her ears, where they dangled like a pair of red ear-rings.

Nella clasped her hands and cried, "Nymph, Nymph, give me my slippers!"

"That I won't!" said the Nymph. "They are *my* slippers, for the Eagle who brings me things brought them to me, and they are the prettiest things I ever saw."

"Then you haven't seen those I wear on my feet," said Nella, and she put out her little feet which happened that day to be shod in her golden slippers. They were much prettier than the red ones, though not nearly so wonderful.

But the Nymph didn't know that, and anyhow she had no use for slippers to dance in, but only to hang in her ears, so she eagerly asked, "Will you change?"

"If you wish it," said Nella. And she kicked off her golden slippers and put on her red ones, while the Blue Nymph hung the golden slippers in her ears, and looked more pleased with herself than before.

"Good-bye," said Nella.

"Good-bye," said the Blue Nymph.

Then Nella rose to the top of the Pool, where the Fan-Man was waiting for her. As soon as he saw her he spread his fan again, and in another moment she was sailing over India and Persia and Turkey and Italy. And when they came to her own rose garden, the Fan-Man stopped, and Nella dropped.

The first thing she did was to stand on her toes and dance.

The next thing she did was to send word to the town, saying, "Tonight I will dance for the Prince of Florence."

And that night, under thousands of stars, amongst thousands of coloured lights, Nella danced on the lawn in her red velvet slippers better than she had ever danced before, and all the people, overjoyed to have their beautiful Nella dancing for them again, climbed on the chairs and the tables, and clapped their hands, shouting:

"*Brava,* Nella! *Brava, brava!*"

X

GOOD-BYE TO ITALY

Anina, who knew how such things should be done, found me one day cooking macaroni. I suppose I was not cooking it in the Italian way, for she came straight to the pot, snatched the spoon from my hand, tasted the Pasta, and spat it out on the floor. Then she pushed me out of the kitchen, and I never dared try to cook again when she was in it. I thought she had a hearty contempt for the work of my hands.

Perhaps she had. But the day I went away she took my hand in her hard, rough one, and kissed it, and called down a blessing on my head, that I might be preserved on my long journey to England. Then she said, "Swear that you will come back to us." And I gave her my promise.

That was long ago; but one day I shall keep it.

XI

THE STORY OF MR AND MRS RINGDALY

I did not make up the story of Mr and Mrs Ringdaly, but I am one of the few people who tell it. I only heard it twice, and the teller told it in his own way, and I tell it in mine. Everybody who tells it is sure to tell it with a difference.

Here is how I tell the story of Mr and Mrs Ringdaly to Bridget, when she is in her nightdress.

ELEANOR: Once upon a time, Bridget, Mr Ringdaly married Mrs Ringdaly, so they gave a Party. Who do you think came to the Party?

BRIDGET: Who?

ELEANOR: Everybody there was! The grandfathers and the grandmothers, the mummies and the daddies, the big boys and the big girls, the little boys and the little girls, and all the babies. And what do you think they wore to the Party?

BRIDGET: What?

ELEANOR: Everything they had! Silks and satins and cottons and rags, laces and ribbons and calico and dimity, woollens and muslins and velvet and sacking, and all the babies came in their nightgowns. And how do you think they came to the Party?

BRIDGET: How?

ELEANOR: In all the ways they could! They came running and riding and walking and sailing, they came in carriages and railway-trains, and on horses and boats and scooters and bicycles and haycarts and fire-engines—

BRIDGET: And aeroplanes?

ELEANOR: And aeroplanes and motor-buses, and all the babies came in their perambulators. And what do you think they had when they got to the Party?

BRIDGET: What?

ELEANOR: Everything there is! They had soups and fishes and meats and vegetables, cakes and puddings and pastries and pies, jellies and creams and custards and tarts, honey and jam and apples and pears and plums and cherries—

BRIDGET: And currants?

ELEANOR: And currants. What do you like best of all?

BRIDGET: And ICE-CREAM?

ELEANOR: And ICE-CREAM! And all the babies had their bottles. *But*—

Not one morsel of any of these things would Mrs Ringdaly touch until they put on the table a dish of rice. And then she took a silver pin, and she stuck it in one grain of rice, and she ate that.

And she stuck it in a Second grain of rice, and she ate *that*!

And she stuck it in a Third grain of rice, and she ate *that*!

And she stuck it in a Fourth grain of rice, and she ate *that*!

And she stuck it in a Fifth grain of rice, and she ate *that*!

And she stuck it in a Sixth grain of rice, and she ate *that*!

And she stuck it in a Seventh grain of rice, and she ate THAT!

And when she had eaten the seventh grain of rice, she ran out of the room and went and sat in the top of a tree.

Well, that made Mr Ringdaly very angry indeed. So he called the Boy and said:

"Boy, go and tell Mrs Ringdaly to come down at once!"

So the Boy went out and stood under the tree and said:

"Mrs Ring - da - ly! Mrs Ring da ly!
The Mas - ter's call - - ing you!"

And Mrs Ringdaly, from the top of the tree, answered:

"Go, Boy! Go, Boy! I can - not
come. There's work to be done . . . at home."

So the Boy went back to Mr Ringdaly and said, "Mrs Ringdaly won't come."

Then Mr Ringdaly was *very* angry indeed, and he said:

"Boy, go and tell Mrs Ringdaly that if she doesn't come down at once I shall come and fetch her myself!"

So the Boy went out again and stood under the tree, and said:

"Mrs Ringdaly!
The Master's calling you!"

And Mrs Ringdaly answered from the top of the tree:

"Go, Boy!
Go, Boy!
I cannot come!
There's work to be done at home."

So the Boy went back to Mr Ringdaly and said, "Mrs Ringdaly won't come."

Then Mr Ringdaly was *very*, VERY angry, and he got his bow and arrow, and went out and stood under the tree himself.

And he said: "Mrs Ringdaly, will you come down Once?"

But Mrs Ringdaly wouldn't come down Once.

Then Mr Ringdaly said: "Mrs Ringdaly, will you come down Twice?"

No, Mrs Ringdaly wouldn't come down Twice.

Then Mr Ringdaly said: "Mrs Ringdaly, will you come down Three Times?"

And no! Mrs Ringdaly wouldn't come down Three Times.

So then, I'm sorry to say, Mr Ringdaly put an arrow to his bow, and he shot it up into the trees; and it shot Mrs Ringdaly right through the heart, and she came fluttering down and down through the leaves till she fell on the ground at his feet.

And what do you think?

BRIDGET: She was a Bird.

That is the story of Mr and Mrs Ringdaly. And though it is one of the saddest stories in the world, Bridget is always rather amused, and rather surprised, because Mrs Ringdaly was a bird all the time. We have never found out why Mr Ringdaly didn't know she was a bird till he shot her, and the story doesn't say what sort of a bird she was.

BRIDGET: She was a Wood-Pigeon.

What do you think?